HOCUS POCUS
HOTEL

Hocus Pocus Hotel is published by Stone Arch Books
A Capstone Imprint
1710 Roe Crest Dr.
North Mankato, Minnesota 56003
www.capstonepub.com

Cataloging-in-Publication Data is available at the Library of Congress website.

ISBN: 978-1-4342-4102-3 (library binding)

Summary: Abracadabra, a mysterious magician, needs Charlie and Tyler's help to save the Abracadabra Hotel.

Photo credits: Shutterstock
Abracadabra Hotel Illustration: Brann Garvey
Designed by Kay Fraser

Printed in China.
082015
009161R

The Trouble with Abracadabra

BY MICHAEL DAHL

ILLUSTRATED BY LISA K. WEBER

STONE ARCH BOOKS™
a capstone imprint

3 THE ABRACADABRA HOTEL

Table of

Contents

An Announcement

Exactly one week after solving the mystery of the missing assistant, Charlie Hitchcock and Tyler Yu stood inside the front doors of the Abracadabra Hotel. The lobby was more crowded than it had been in decades.

"Wow," said Charlie. "What's going on?"

As a permanent resident of the hotel, Ty should know why the place was packed. But the big guy just shrugged. "Beats me," he said. "I'll try to find my mom."

While Ty weaved through the crowd to try to reach the registration desk, Charlie tried snooping around. He slipped behind a big marble column and listened to a few people talking. "Any idea what the big news is?" asked a woman in a suit.

"Nope," a man replied. He had a camera around his neck. "We got a call at the paper this morning, and I came right down."

Another man walked up in a hurry. "They're calling us in," he said, out of breath. "Come on. Let's get a seat in front."

The three people ran off toward the dining room off the lobby.

"Reporters," Charlie said to himself.

The crowd in the lobby streamed toward the dining room. Charlie spotted a bunch of other people who he thought must be reporters. The rest of them seemed like they might be magicians.

"I can't find my mom," said Ty, walking up. "I don't know what's going on."

"Well, whatever's going on," Charlie said, "it's going on in there." He pointed to the dining room.

"Then let's go," said Ty. The boys hurried in just before the doors were closed.

The tables were gone. At the front of the big room was a stage. A microphone stood in the center. Hundreds of chairs had been set up. Reporters and photographers filled the chairs and lined the walls and aisles too. Men and women in tuxedoes and Gypsy clothes and jester costumes were also sprinkled through the crowd.

Charlie whispered, "How did they all find out about this?"

"This must be how," Ty said. He bent over and grabbed a sheet of paper from the carpeted floor.

BIG NEWS!

THIS ANNOUNCEMENT WILL BE THE MOST IMPORTANT NEWS TO THE WORLD OF MAGIC! ALL PRESS AND PHOTOGRAPHERS INVITED!

ALL MAGICIANS URGED TO MAKE AN APPEARANCE! ABRACADABRA HOTEL, 11 A.M. ON THE DOT!

Just then, the lights dimmed in the dining room and a spotlight shined on the lectern. "Here goes," said Charlie.

And it was just as he suspected. From the side door next to the little stage, out came Brack, the elevator operator of the hotel. Secretly, Brack was Abracadabra himself: the founder and owner of the hotel. Only Charlie knew that, though.

"What's he doing?" Ty said.

"Thank you all for coming," said Brack, smiling at the crowd. "I'm sure you're wondering why I've called you all here this morning," he said.

A reporter in the front raised his hand and shouted, "*You* called us? We thought it was something important."

"Yeah!" someone else called out. "You're just the elevator man!"

"Ah," said Brack. He removed his hat. "That is what I've come to talk to you about. I am not just the elevator operator."

"He also scrubs the toilets," joked a magician along the wall. Charlie scowled.

Brack cleared his throat at the microphone. Then he raised both hands in a high wide arc over his head. He threw back his head and shouted, "Abracadabra!"

A great puff of smoke came up from the stage floor. The lights flickered and flashed in the dining room. When the smoke cleared, Brack was gone.

A moment later, the lights flashed on for a second. Thunder crashed through the room. The walls and chairs shook. And then, from the high ceiling over the stage, smoke and light fell. Then came a man. He wore a red and green robe and a shining silver crown set in a big colorful turban.

As his feet touched the stage, he raised his arms and smiled.

"I am Brack," he announced, "and I am Abracadabra! Be back here one week from tonight for my first show in fifty years!"

Thunder clapped again. Lightning struck across the ceiling. The crowd gasped.

Flashes went off. Hands went into the air. Frenzied reporters shouted out questions and demands. Magicians rushed the stage.

The place went, in a word, nuts.

* * *

It was an hour before the conference room and lobby were cleared out. While they waited for the craziness to die down, Charlie and Ty sat on one of the red velvet couches near the front desk.

"I can't believe it," Ty said.

Charlie grinned. "I already knew," he said.

Ty stared at him. "You're kidding me," he said.

"Nope," Charlie said. "I figured it out, and Brack confirmed it." He reached into his pocket and pulled out his golden ticket. "And I'm invited to the final performance."

Ty narrowed his eyes. "I better be too," he muttered.

"I'm sure I can bring a guest," Charlie said, and winked.

The Little Golden Key

Many of the magicians who attended the announcement had decided to get rooms at the hotel. The line to check in was getting long.

Just then, a big group of reporters came shuffling across the lobby. The reporters were moving in a tight group. They were shouting questions.

"I think they have Brack," said Ty.

The group of reporters moved right at the boys. Soon it engulfed them.

"What tricks will you do?" one reporter shouted.

"Oh," said Brack when he saw Charlie and Ty. Brack was in his elevator-operator uniform again. His face showed the stress his announcement had created. "Hello, you two," he said.

"Why have you been in hiding?" another reporter said.

"*Where* have you been hiding?" one more asked. Ty rolled his eyes.

"What's going on?" Charlie asked Brack. He had to shout to be heard over the gaggle of reporters. He struggled to shuffle along inside the ambling crowd.

"Why are you retiring from magic, after being gone all these years?" said another reporter.

"Follow my lead," Brack said to Charlie and Ty. He shuffled one way, and the crowd followed. Ty and Charlie shuffled along with him.

"He's heading for the elevator," Ty muttered to Charlie.

Ty was right. When they got very close to the elevator bank, Brack put a hand on the boys' collars, stepped backward into the open elevator, and then quickly closed the door. The reporters were stuck on the other side.

"Whew," Brack said, taking off his hat. "I knew this would cause a ruckus, but I wasn't prepared for so much attention." He shook his head slowly.

He pulled keys from his pocket — he had a lot of keys — and flipped through them until he found a very small golden one. Then he raised the keys to a tiny door on the elevator control panel.

"I never noticed that before," Ty said.

On the little door was a keyhole. Brack used his little golden key, turned it to the right, and the elevator started going up.

"A secret floor," said Ty in a hushed, sacred voice.

He looked over at Charlie and narrowed his eyes. "Did you know about this?" he asked.

Charlie glanced at Brack, who had a twinkle in his eye.

"Uh, yeah," Charlie said.

"I can't believe it, Hitch," Ty said. "I can't believe it!"

For a second, Charlie saw a glimmer of the old Ty — the biggest bully in school, not his friend.

But then Brack said, calmly, "I asked Master Hitchcock to not say anything to you, Master Yu. I wanted to tell you myself, you see. The problem was, time ran out. I'm very sorry."

"Oh, that's okay, Brack," Ty said. "I get it." He narrowed his eyes at Charlie again, but the angry look was gone.

The elevator climbed and climbed. The dial above the door swung slowly, higher and higher. It went past the top floor and kept going.

Ty looked at Brack quizzically, but he just smiled and watched the dial climb.

Finally, the elevator stopped. A bell dinged. The doors slid open.

"Whoa," said Ty. He stood there, dumbfounded, as Brack stepped out.

Before them was Brack's house on the roof. "Pretty cool, huh?" Charlie whispered.

"Uh, yeah," Ty said. "I can't believe I never knew this was here."

"Welcome to my home," Brack said. He walked up the front path toward the big wooden doors of the mansion. "Please, follow me."

Inside, Brack headed straight to the kitchen, a sunny room at the back of the house.

"Have a seat, you two," Brack said. "We've a lot to discuss."

"What's on your mind, Brack?" Ty asked. He flipped around a chair and sat down. "Should we call you Abracadabra now?"

Brack laughed. "Don't be silly," he said. "Why, if anyone calls me Abracadabra, I'll know to keep my guard up."

"What do you mean?" Charlie asked as he sat down at the table.

Brack sighed and sipped his tea. "For a long time," he said, "I was the most famous magician in the city, maybe in the country."

"Pff," said Ty. "You were the biggest magician in the world, probably ever."

"Perhaps," said Brack. "When I founded this hotel, though, I became quite an attraction. That much is certain. For many years, young magicians from all over the world wanted to share the stage with me."

"Sure," Charlie said. "Who wouldn't?"

Brack nodded. "At first, I was honored," he said. "But then it became clear: most of these young magicians were just looking to grab their own piece of fame. They didn't respect me. They didn't care about me at all."

"Harsh," said Ty.

"Indeed, it wasn't long before a new breed of magician began showing up, right here at the hotel," said Brack. "These were true cutthroats. If it would help their careers to take me down a notch, or eliminate me entirely, all the better. They'd stop at nothing to achieve their greedy goals."

"At first I tried to help," Brack went on. "Soon it became too hard. When many tried to take advantage of me, or even try to put me down or set me up for failure, I realized I could so easily just disappear."

"Poof!" Ty said. He snapped his fingers.

Brack chuckled. "Not quite like that," he said. "That's how I would have done it in a magic show, of course: in a grand puff of smoke, like at this morning's press conference. But I had something different in mind."

"So you became Brack," Charlie said. "The mild-mannered elevator operator."

"Precisely," Brack said. He frowned. "Now that I'm back, those fame-hungry magicians will begin hounding me at any moment. This time, I'm ready for them." He lifted a card from the table and passed it to Ty.

"I sent these out yesterday," Brack said. "Every magician in the country will be getting his or her invitation today."

You are cordially invited to

ABRACADABRA'S ROOF-TOP MANSION

at the hotel that bears his name

Ty looked at Brack, his eyes wide. "You're inviting them?" he asked. "I thought you didn't want to see these people!"

"Oh, I can't stop them from showing up," Brack said. "But this way, I will have the upper hand in two ways."

"Which ways?" Charlie asked.

"One, they will all be here at once," Brack said. "They'll spend all their time trying to impress each other and knock each other down. They won't pester me."

"And two?" Charlie said.

"Ah," said Brack, smiling. "That's where you boys come in."

Ty and Charlie leaned forward.

"The party is tomorrow night," Brack said. "And you're both very important parts of it."

"Us?" said Charlie. "We're not magicians."

"Indeed," said Brack. He stood up and brought his teacup to the sink. "That's why I know I can count on you two to keep an eye on everyone else."

Filthy with Magicians

The next twenty-four hours were a flurry of activity in the hotel. All the magicians had checked in.

Now that the invitations had arrived, the magical guests gabbed and gossiped in the lobby for hours at a time. They had lunch in the hotel restaurant. They milled around the hotel games room, chatting about what tricks they'd show off at the party.

Meanwhile, the reporters were back. Word had gotten out, and it seemed like a big scoop.

Especially Abracadabra's performance at the magic show. He'd been gone so long, there was little doubt among the reporters that he had some new amazing tricks up his silk sleeves.

One reporter in particular hung around the lobby a lot — usually right next to Charlie. His name was Joey Bingham.

It was early Sunday morning. The party was that night, and there was a lot of work to do. Charlie and Ty were behind the lobby desk when Joey walked up. "How did you know Brack the elevator operator was actually Abracadabra?" he asked.

"I told you, Joey," Charlie said. "I figured it out."

Charlie and Ty knew Joey. Not long ago, he'd investigated the disappearance of a classmate with them — though he didn't contribute much to the investigation. For a reporter, he seemed pretty clueless.

Joey shook his head. "I find it hard to believe," he said, "that you two would figure out this great secret."

"Why?" said Ty. "We're smart. I happen to be very intelligent, and Charlie is a total whiz at remembering stuff and figuring stuff out."

Joey smirked. "Of course you are," he said. He leaned close to the boys and said in a whisper, "But the rest of us are professional reporters. We investigate and discover secrets for a living."

"You couldn't find the missing boy," Charlie said quickly.

Joey's face went red. "I would have," he said. "Eventually."

"Anyway, we have to help Mr. Abracadabra set up for the party," said Ty. He grabbed Charlie's arm to pull him away. "We're his friends, you know."

Joey sneered at them as they walked off. Then he gasped at something behind them.

The rest of the lobby — full of magicians and reporters — gasped too. Ty and Charlie turned and saw flashes go off. The reporters began to run for the front door as it swung closed. Smiling and posing for the hundreds of cameras on him was the Great Theopolis — the very magician and illusionist who had been responsible for the missing boy that Joey Bingham couldn't find.

Joey ran toward the door with the others. Charlie and Ty stayed back to watch.

They leaned against the registration desk. Annie leaned on the desk from the other side. "I thought he checked out," Charlie said.

Annie said, "He did. I guess he's back. He'll want his room on the thirteenth floor again, I guess." She started shuffling through the room cards and keys. "He always stays there."

"He was probably invited to the big party," said Charlie.

Ty nodded. "And after his big stunt with the disappearing kid," he said, "Theopolis is the most famous magician in town."

"He *was* the most famous magician in town, you mean," said Charlie with a smirk. "Now Brack is."

"And I bet Theopolis isn't too happy about that," Ty said. "We'll have to keep a close eye on him."

* * *

Theopolis and Joey Bingham weren't the only familiar faces to arrive at the Abracadabra Hotel that day.

Charlie also spotted Professor Pontificate, the mind reader and mind controller, strolling around the lobby. And, he saw, there was Mr. Madagascar, a master of levitation and long-time resident of the hotel who hardly ever left his room. Today, though, he was in the lobby with the rest of the crowd, along with his friend Dotty Drake. She'd been a great magician's assistant in the old days.

Then there was Madame Krzyscky, the fire-eater from the theater's premier show the week before. She wore a glittery skin-tight costume in red, orange, and yellow. She looked like fire herself as she walked around the lobby.

Ty elbowed Charlie in the side and pointed across the lobby. Charlie's eyes went wide. Objects were flying through the air over the heads of the crowd in the lobby. He saw a bowling pin. He saw a baseball, a basketball, and a tennis racquet. He gasped when he saw a flaming stick, and then another.

Finally the objects stopped flying. A few people — reporters, mostly — applauded. The crowd parted and Charlie could see now: it was Mr. Thursday, master juggler.

A few weeks earlier, Charlie and Ty had thought Mr. Thursday was a ghost.

He'd been practicing his routine for a big comeback show in the hotel's old theater. Little did they know then that the magicians were running a kind of dress rehearsal for the big reappearance of Abracadabra.

"I guess everyone's here," said Ty.

Charlie looked around the lobby. There were other jugglers. There were jesters. There were magicians' assistants — mostly women, but some men — of all ages, wearing leotards or long white gowns or silver sequined bodysuits. There were plenty of men in tuxedoes and top hats, sometimes even with bunnies popping out of them. There were all sorts of card tricks going on. There were even people floating up near the ceiling, showing off their levitation tricks.

The place was absolutely filthy with magicians.

"And just think," Charlie said. He crossed his arms. "Each and every one of them will be at Brack's party tonight."

True Magic

It was a warm night, so most of the partygoers stayed outside. They sat on the benches in the rooftop garden. They lounged on the chairs next to the rooftop pool.

Brack started the night standing on his own, wearing a simple brown suit. Charlie and Ty stood not far off, so they could keep an eye on him.

But before long, he'd been spotted, sitting at a table under a canopy.

"Hey, there's the old master," said a magician. It only took seconds before Brack's table was mobbed.

Magicians stood in front of his table. They made things disappear. They made things appear. They juggled. They levitated objects and levitated themselves. The assistants performed flourishes or little spins, showing off their clothes or hair or smile.

At the table, Brack smiled politely.

"Do you have an open slot in your farewell show, Mr. Abracadabra?" asked a woman after she made her sister disappear — and then reappear as her brother.

"Please, Mr. Abracadabra," said a man as he juggled bowling balls while riding a unicycle, "make room for me on that stage!"

Brack didn't respond to anyone. He just smiled.

Theopolis was the last magician to arrive. He strode off the elevator, right up the front path. Then he stomped to the front of the line of magicians.

Tonight he wore his most impressive garb: a heavy black robe that shined like silk, trimmed with silver and gold thread. He carried a staff, like some ancient wizard. On each side of him was a magician's assistant, both hobbled and bent. The assistants were dressed in burlap cloaks.

Charlie elbowed Ty, who was busy watching some jugglers practicing next to the pool.

"Look who's here," Charlie said.

Theopolis threw back the hood of his robe.

At the same moment, a huge bolt of lightning — one of Theopolis's special effects — struck his wizard's staff. Smoke rose up from his feet.

"Wow," said Ty. "You have to admit, he knows how to make an entrance."

"Mr. Abracadabra!" Theopolis said in his deepest voice. "I — the Great and Powerful Theopolis, lord of the demon realm and the greatest sorcerer in the dimension — have come to offer a challenge."

Brack winked at Ty and Charlie. Then he looked back at Theopolis. "Go on," he said.

A few people nearby chuckled. Theopolis ignored them. "This hotel has become old," Theopolis said, putting up his arms grandly. "You have become old."

Brack shrugged and smiled. "Too true," he said.

"Your retirement from magic," said Theopolis, "draws near. You will no doubt enjoy a rest. A very long rest. It will do you good."

"He's been resting for fifty years," Ty whispered to Charlie.

"The hotel itself could use some fixing too," Theopolis went on. "Its age is showing, as yours is. It needs to be . . . updated. Brought up to modern times." He laughed. "You've been in hiding for a long time, old man. The world has changed, and so has magic."

"Perhaps," said Brack.

"And so, I offer this challenge," Theopolis said. "I will now perform an act of magic so striking, so amazing, that you will not believe it possible."

"An illusion?" Brack said.

"No illusion," said Theopolis. "True magic — the demonic power I learned in my studies. Power from other dimensions."

"I see," said Brack. "Then what is the challenge?"

"I say it is magic," Theopolis said. "You say it is an illusion. Then prove it. After the feat, you will have until the night of your final performance to show how it was done."

"And if I can't?" Brack said.

"Ah," said Theopolis. He grinned and made a temple of his fingers before his face. "If you cannot, then you back out of your final performance and hand the theater over to me . . . and the hotel along with it."

The Power

"What?!" said Charlie.

"That's ridiculous!" shouted Ty.

Brack put up his hand to silence the boys. "What if I do show how it was done?" Brack asked Theopolis. "What will you give me?"

Theopolis frowned in disdain. "It's barely worth considering," he said, "but if that happens, I suppose we can come to some monetary agreement."

"No money," Brack said. "You will agree never to step foot inside this hotel again."

"Very well," said Theopolis. He bowed.

Brack stood up from his chair and walked out from behind the table. He didn't look like the old elevator operator today. He didn't look old at all, except in the way that a tall and mighty oak tree looks old.

Brack stood in front of Theopolis. They were about the same height when Brack stood fully upright. "Begin your trick, Theo," Brack said. He didn't smile.

"It's no trick," said Theopolis.

"Yes, yes," Brack said. "It's true magic. Just get on with it."

Theopolis bowed deeply, smiling. With a flourish of his black robe, he walked to the far side of the pool. He pushed through the crowds.

For a moment, Charlie lost sight of him. Then Theopolis reappeared at the edge of the pool. He walked to the end of the diving board and stopped.

Ty and Charlie shuffled over to stand with Brack. "You boys watch closely," Brack said out of the side of his mouth. "You can bet Theopolis won't make this easy."

Charlie nodded. He and Ty had solved one of Theopolis's tricks already. Maybe this wouldn't be so hard.

* * *

Any hopes Charlie and Ty had that this trick would be as simple as Theopolis's last trick were dashed right away.

Theopolis was in prime form. Thick white smoke rose up from the ground and settled over the roof.

Theopolis threw back his head and raised his staff with both hands. Thunder clapped across the sky. Party guests flinched and ran for cover under canopies and on the mansion's big front porch. Only Brack, Charlie, and Ty stayed beside the pool.

The whole rooftop estate filled with an eerie red light. The light crackled and popped, like tiny bolts of lightning.

"Great demons of the dimensions of power!" Theopolis shouted at the thundering red sky. "I call upon you! Give me your power!"

As he spoke, the thunder grew louder. The sky became a deeper, darker red. The lights at the party — which had been so bright and friendly — switched off.

Suddenly the rooftop party looked less like a celebration of Abracadabra's return and more like the vision from a nightmare.

"Give me the power!" Theopolis screamed at the sky once more.

Then, slowly at first, he rose from the diving board. He kept his head and arms up to the sky, and he rose higher and higher, until he was at least twenty feet over the pool.

Magicians gasped and muttered. Assistants sighed and clapped. Charlie and Tyler looked at each other, and then stared back at Theopolis.

But Theopolis wasn't done yet.

High above the rooftop, the robed figure floated farther out over the pool. He brought down the staff and lowered his head for a moment. The crowd hushed.

Suddenly, Theopolis threw the staff straight up, into the dark red sky and the white clouds of smoke and the streaks of lightning.

Charlie knew that all of it — the smoke, the thunder, the lightning — was just special effects. Still, he couldn't help being impressed. Theopolis might be a fame-hungry, underhanded jerk, but he was good at putting on a show.

The staff reached its apex and seemed to explode. When it fell back toward Theopolis, who was still floating high above the swimming pool, it was in three pieces.

The Great Theopolis didn't flinch. He caught the three pieces and immediately tossed them up.

Before Charlie could guess what had happened, Theopolis was juggling the three pieces perfectly.

The crowd cheered. Brack nodded, impressed. Ty leaned closer to Charlie and whispered, "Since when does Theopolis juggle?"

Charlie shrugged. It was a good question.

Finally, Theopolis caught all three pieces at once. The staff seemed to reassemble itself. He held it aloft once more. "I thank you, great demons of the dimensions!" he shouted into the clouds. "And now, go back to your own realm!"

Lightning cracked. The thunder boomed: the loudest crash yet. Charlie had to cover his ears with his hands. The red light flashed brightly, and Charlie had to turn away and close his eyes.

When Charlie looked back, Theopolis was gone.

"Where'd he go?" someone shouted.

Chattering spread through the crowd of magicians and assistants. Most of them sounded very impressed. A few magicians standing near Brack and the boys said things like, "Pff, I could do that," and, "I don't see what the big deal is."

But it *was* a big deal, Charlie knew. Theopolis had levitated, called demons from another dimension, controlled the weather, and vanished.

He'd even *juggled*.

Brack put his arms around Ty and Charlie. "I hope you boys were watching closely," he said quietly. "I'll need your help to figure this one out."

Just then, someone stepped up behind them. "Counting on the help of two children?" said Theopolis. He laughed. "This proves it. You are too old, too out of touch with magic today."

Brack didn't respond.

"You have less than one week," Theopolis said. "Then you will leave this theater, cancel your farewell show, and hand over this hotel — and this rooftop estate — to me."

He pulled up his hood, sneering at Charlie and Ty, and stormed for the exit.

"What a nasty man," Charlie said.

Brack nodded. "Indeed," he said, "but he is also a master illusionist."

"What are you saying?" Ty asked.

"I'm saying that I hope you two have some ideas," Brack said, "because frankly I'm stumped." With that, the old magician walked back to his table under the canopy.

THEOPOLIS'S TRICK

THEOPOLIS levitating
and juggling

Pool

Full Reboot

The next day was Monday, so Charlie
and Ty had to get back to school. Charlie
had a load of homework he hadn't done
over the weekend, so for the next two days,
he was stuck at home after school.

He didn't get back to the hotel until
Wednesday afternoon.

"Have you figured anything out?" Charlie asked Ty when he arrived at the Abracadabra.

"Of course not," Ty said. He was lounging on the couch nearest the front desk. He nodded toward the elevators.

Charlie turned to look. There was Brack, wearing his elevator-operator uniform. He was sitting in his chair in the lobby right by the elevators. He didn't look happy.

"He's been like that since the party, pretty much," Ty said. "I think he's just hoping Theopolis will let him stay on as elevator operator when he gives him the hotel."

Charlie shook his head sadly. "He's really given up already?" he asked.

"Can you blame him?" Ty said.

Just then, the front doors of the hotel swung open and Theopolis entered.

And so did a lot of other people.

Charlie recognized some of the assistants from the party. They trailed close behind him. There were a few magicians from the party too, including Mr. Thursday, the juggling expert.

And behind the whole group of magic people were reporters. They barked questions and took photos and shot video.

Theopolis led the little parade, his face full of pride. When he reached the center of the lobby — where he could be easily seen by everyone, including Brack — he stopped.

"Ladies and gentlemen," Theopolis said, smiling smugly, "I will answer all your questions. Now, who is first?"

Joey Bingham stepped up and held out his microphone. "What are your plans for the hotel when you take it over?" he asked.

"See?" said Ty quietly to Charlie. "Everyone's acting like Brack already lost."

Theopolis made a big show of looking up and around the lobby. "So much wasted space," he said. Then he ran a finger along the back of a nearby lobby chair. "And everything is so old."

He pretended his finger was dirty just from having rubbed the chair. The reporters chuckled.

Charlie glanced at Brack. The old magician hung his head.

"My plan is a full reboot, if you follow me," Theopolis said. He walked toward the elevators as he spoke. "I will modernize everything. There will be projectors, flat-panel screens all over the lobby. There will be a fully demon staff, naturally."

"Naturally," grunted Ty sarcastically.

"We'll start by tearing up the old theater," Theopolis said, just as he and his group reached the elevators. "Now excuse me. I will go up to my room."

Without even looking at Brack, he barked out, "Thirteenth floor, please." Then he stepped into the elevator with his two hobbled assistants. Brack got up with a sigh and stepped into the elevator too. The doors closed.

Charlie gritted his teeth. "It's time for us to get to work," he said.

Ty nodded. "Where do we start?"

"First, we talk to Rocky," Charlie said.

"He's in the office," Ty said, slipping behind the front desk. "Come on."

Charlie followed. Soon the two boys were sitting in the main office. Rocky, one of the front-desk workers, leaned on a file cabinet.

"So," Charlie said, "are you with us?"

"Sure," said Rocky. "I don't want Brack to lose the hotel either. Can you imagine working for that nut Theopolis? No way. So, how can I help?"

"Give us a list of every magician who's checked into the hotel since Brack's press conference," Charlie said.

"Why do we want that?" Ty asked.

"They were all at the party," Charlie said, "and they're all experts in magic, to some degree. Maybe one of them can help us."

"Coming right up," Rocky said. He went to the front desk and started tapping at the computer.

"What if they won't help us?" Ty said.

Charlie thought about it. "I don't know," he said, "but right now, what else can we do?"

The Best Juggler Around

Ty and Charlie talked to magicians all afternoon and into the evening. Charlie had to call home and tell his parents he'd miss dinner. It was late when they got to Mr. Thursday, the juggler, and they weren't even halfway down the list yet.

Ty knocked on the door of room 1001. The juggler opened the door immediately.

"Yes?" he said. "Oh, it's you two. Come on in." He moved back inside and left the door open for them.

The room was a mess, strewn with bowling pins and bowling balls, softballs and baseballs, unlit torches, knives and batons. "I was just in the middle of practicing," Thursday said. "I'm always in the middle of practicing, actually."

"We won't take up too much of your time," Charlie said. "We're asking everyone who was at the party if they have thoughts about Theopolis's big trick."

"Helping out old man Brack, huh?" Mr. Thursday said. He sat down on the couch.

"We're trying to," Ty said. He sat down too. "We've already talked to a hundred magicians."

"Well, maybe ten," Charlie said.

"Whatever," said Ty. "The point is we still have no idea how Theopolis did that stuff."

Mr. Thursday's eyebrows went up. "No idea at all?" he asked.

Charlie shook his head.

"Well, the juggling was very good," Mr. Thursday said. "In fact, it was some of the best juggling I've ever seen in my life."

"Really?" said Ty. "That's surprising to hear. You're the best juggler around. I wouldn't think you'd be so quick to praise Theopolis. Is he a friend of yours?"

"Of course not," Thursday said with a chuckle. "I've never even talked to him. I just think his juggling was very good."

"Especially since he was floating in midair," added Charlie.

Mr. Thursday stood up.

"I don't know anything about that," he said. "I'm no levitation expert." He moved toward the door. "Now, if you two will excuse me," he said. "I have a lot of practicing to do."

Ty stood up. "Do you have a performance coming up?" he asked.

"If everything goes according to plan," Mr. Thursday said, "yes."

Charlie and Ty stepped into the hallway. Mr. Thursday closed the door.

Ty sighed. "That was no help at all," he said, glancing at the list. "Let's see, who's next?"

Charlie yawned. "I have to get home," he said. "Let's pick this up tomorrow after school."

"Okay," said Ty. "Three o'clock. Don't be late."

Slamhammer!

The next day of school was the longest Charlie had ever experienced. As soon as the last bell rang, he hurried to the hotel.

Ty was already there. "Finally," said the bigger boy when Charlie ran into the lobby, out of breath. "What took you so long?"

"How . . . how did you get here so fast?" Charlie asked.

Ty laughed. "Take a guess," he said. "What's quicker than walking? In fact, what's as fast as . . . lightning?"

Charlie gasped. "You got it?" he said. "You got your bike?"

Grinning, Ty pulled it out from behind the front desk: the Tezuki Slamhammer 750, Edition 6, in cherry-pop lightning red.

"That's amazing," Charlie said, staring at the beautiful bike. "Nice work."

"Okay," said Ty. "Enough ogling. Let's get started."

Mr. Madagascar frowned when he opened the door. "What do you two want?" he asked. He was in a ratty old bathrobe. His room was a complete mess. There were at least a dozen mirrors of all sizes leaning against the walls and furniture.

"Were you at the party the other night?" Ty asked. "The one at Brack's rooftop estate."

"Of course I was," Mr. M. said. "Every magician in the city was there."

"Did you see the trick?" Charlie asked.

"Theopolis's trick?" Madagascar asked. He leaned on the open doorway.

He hasn't invited us in, Charlie thought.

"Yes, I saw it," Mr. M. said. "It was very impressive, wasn't it? The levitation was very good. Over water? Difficult business. But you two wouldn't understand."

"That good, huh?" Charlie said. "I didn't know Theopolis was an expert in levitation."

Mr. Madagascar squinted at the boy. "Yes," he said slowly, in a very rough voice. "I didn't know either."

"But you were impressed?" Charlie asked.

"Quite," said Mr. Madagascar. Just then, someone cleared her throat behind the boys, and Charlie spun around.

It was Dotty Drake, Mr. Madagascar's assistant.

Mr. Madagascar looked at the boys. "Now you'll have to excuse us. Dotty and I are about to rehearse our act."

"Do you have a show soon?" Charlie asked.

"Ah, nothing scheduled yet, exactly," Madagascar said. "But we're very hopeful."

Then Dotty closed the door in their faces.

Four Magicians in One

The boys spent the rest of the afternoon and evening talking to other magicians. No one was especially helpful. It was nearly eight before they gave up for the night again.

Charlie leaned against the front counter and yawned. "I guess I better get home," he said.

Tyler nodded. "We only have a couple more days," he said. "I'm losing hope."

Just then, Brack stepped out of the elevator and plodded across the lobby.

"Brack!" Charlie and Ty shouted. They ran over to him.

"Where have you been?" Charlie asked. "We've hardly seen you since the party."

Brack looked tired. He sat down on a bench and considered the boys. "I've been hard at work," he said.

"Rehearsing for the big farewell show?" Ty asked.

Brack sighed. "Why waste my time with that?" he said. "If I lose this bet, there won't be a farewell show." He put his hands on his knees and sat up straighter. "No," he said, "I've been trying to duplicate Theopolis's trick."

"Any luck?" Charlie asked. "We could use your insight."

"Put it this way," Brack said, smiling. "I'm wearing my elevator-operator outfit because all my other clothes are upstairs hanging out to dry."

"Fell in the pool a few times?" Ty asked.

"Try ten times," Brack said. He chuckled, and then sighed. "I'll miss this place."

Charlie put a hand on Brack's shoulder. "We'll figure it out, Mr. Abracadabra," he said. "I promise."

But Brack didn't seem to be listening. He shook his head sadly. "I just can't figure it out," he said. "Juggling, levitation, special effects, vanishing . . . it's like four magicians rolled into one."

He sighed. Then he got up and headed for the break room.

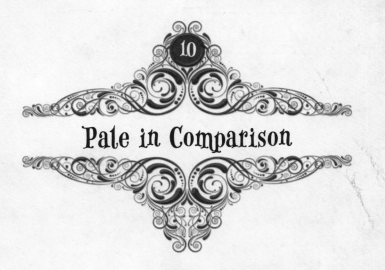

Pale in Comparison

Charlie hardly slept for the next two nights. On Saturday, he knew he should go down to the Abracadabra Hotel for some last-minute investigating, but he couldn't bear to.

There's no point, Charlie thought. *I might as well stay in bed and watch TV all day.*

But that evening, the phone rang at Charlie's house. It was Ty.

"Why aren't you here?" Ty asked.

"Why should I be?" Charlie said. "It's over. Theopolis won. Even Brack can't figure it out."

"Don't be such a wuss," Ty said. "Besides, I *have* figured it out."

Charlie sat up and pushed the blanket to the floor. "What do you mean?" he asked.

"It was something Brack said the other night, right before you left," Ty said. "'Four magicians rolled into one.'"

Charlie scratched his head. "What do you mean?" he asked.

"I'll explain when you get down here," Ty said, and he hung up.

* * *

Charlie was dressed and heading for the hotel in no time flat. If Ty was right, there was only a little time left to solve the mystery and stop Theopolis from ruining Brack's farewell show — and taking the hotel. He ran the whole way.

At the Abracadabra, the lobby was totally packed, just like it had been a week before.

Then he realized that many of the magicians were in costume, as if they were going to perform. He spotted Mr. Thursday, in his finest tuxedo. He was hauling his case of juggling objects.

And there, by the big window along the front wall, were Mr. Madagascar and Dotty. Mr. M. was in fancy robes, ready to put on a show. Dotty was in her old-time magician's assistant outfit: a leotard and high-heeled shoes.

Over by the box office, Charlie saw Theopolis. As usual, a group of hangers-on and reporters surrounded him. Among them was Ty.

Charlie hurried over. "What are you doing?" he hissed, tugging on Ty's maroon jacket sleeve.

Ty shushed him. Then he raised his hand and called out, "Mr. Theopolis, sir?"

The crowd hushed. Ty's voice was loud enough to be heard over all the reporters.

"Who said that?" Theopolis said, looking around. "Oh," he said when he spotted Ty. "What do you want?"

"Well, sir," Ty said. Charlie could tell he was doing his best not to smile. "You're all dressed for a show tonight," Ty went on. "But you're not on the marquee outside the hotel. Mr. Abracadabra is."

"If your old friend Brack hasn't shown the illusion in my performance at his party by now," Theopolis said, "I don't think he will in the next thirty minutes."

"I think I see what you're getting at," Charlie whispered to Ty. Then he said out loud to Theopolis, "Will you share the stage with any other performers?"

"Of course," said Theopolis haughtily. "I never perform alone. Other magicians are helpful for getting the crowd warmed up."

He smiled hugely and looked out over the faces of reporters nearby. "Of course," he added, "since I'm the greatest magician to ever live, they can't help but pale in comparison to me. They agree to join me because they know I can lift them to greatness." The press laughed and cheered. Theopolis's assistants clapped and threw flower petals over him.

But not everyone was cheering. Charlie looked for Mr. Madagascar. The levitationist's face was bent in an angry scowl, and his arms were crossed over his chest.

Mr. Thursday was standing there too. He held a bowling pin in one hand and slapped it into his other hand over and over.

"If looks could kill, huh?" Ty said, nodding toward Mr. Thursday.

Charlie sighed. Dotty Drake was between the two men, with her hands on her hips. She shifted and glared at Theopolis as the press cheered for him.

"We better find Brack," Charlie said. "He only has a few minutes to win this bet."

"And I know how he can do it," Ty added.

Assistance

"I had a hunch we'd find you here," Ty called as he and Charlie stepped off the elevator.

Brack stood up from his spot beneath a tree on the Abracadabra's roof. "How did you two get up here?" he said, but he didn't seem angry.

Ty held up his key ring. "Turns out Rocky had the extra key," he said.

Brack shrugged. "I had to make a copy for emergencies," he said. "Are you here to say good-bye?"

"Of course not," Charlie said. "But we have to hurry and get downstairs before the show starts."

"Right," said Ty. "You've got to get on that stage and announce that you've won the bet."

"I haven't," Brack said sadly. "I'm sorry, boys. I don't know how he did it."

"We do," Ty said.

"We'll explain everything on the way down," said Charlie.

* * *

The theater was packed. Every seat was full, and some people were even standing up behind the back rows, even way up in the balcony.

When Brack stepped into the theater with Charlie and Ty, he practically bumped into Theopolis. The demonic magician in his black robe stood near the doors with his assistants. He was waiting, it seemed, for the wager deadline to arrive.

"Brack," he said through a toothy grin. "How noble of you to come down to the theater, despite your failure."

Brack put out his hand to shake and Theopolis accepted.

The crowd grew silent. Charlie could feel the people around him straining to hear the conversation between the two great illusionists.

"You are a wise man," Theopolis said. "You have lost with grace. And since you're here, you've saved me the considerable trouble of sending security to remove you from my new rooftop estate."

Brack smiled, and then he continued his walk down the aisle toward the stage. Charlie and Ty hurried after him.

"Where do you think you're going?" Theopolis hollered after them. "You won't be taking that stage tonight, nor ever again!"

Brack did not stop. He took the steps up the stage. Theopolis tried to follow, but Charlie and Ty stepped in front of him, blocking his path.

"Out of my way, children," Theopolis said. "This theater belongs to me. I shall have you thrown out!" He thrust his finger in the air as he spoke.

"It's not yours yet," said Charlie. He checked his watch. "Brack has ten minutes."

Ty smirked. "Why don't you take a seat?" he said. "I'm sure Brack would be happy to give you his box seat in the front."

"Yeah. He won't need it!" Charlie said.

The boys laughed and Theopolis steamed.

A stagehand hurried to push out a lectern. There was some hurried chatter in the wings and in the catwalk, and a spotlight thumped on.

"Ladies and gentlemen," Brack said, "and children of all ages. I have a couple of announcements."

The crowd went silent.

"First of all, the performance tonight will not be as scheduled," Brack said.

Theopolis smiled. "A concession speech," he said. He smirked at Charlie and Ty. "Such class."

"It will in fact begin a few minutes late," Brack went on. "I haven't dressed yet, as you can see."

"What?" Theopolis snapped.

"And the second announcement," Brack said, "I only have a few minutes to complete. I shall now reveal how Theopolis performed his levitation trick — yes, *trick*, not magic — at my party last weekend."

Theopolis gasped. "Impossible!" he said. "Get down from that stage at once!"

Ty and Charlie held Theopolis's arms to stop him from rushing the stage.

"I would like some assistance, however," Brack said. "I will ask three excellent performers to join me onstage. I think they're here in the theater."

The crowd of magicians began to chatter. It could be any three of them, they hoped.

"Expert juggler, Mr. Thursday," Brack said. Mr. Thursday stood up in the back row and the crowd applauded slightly.

"Mr. Madagascar," Brack said, "the brilliant levitator and illusionist!"

Mr. Madagascar, who was seated along the wall near the front, stood up. The crowd applauded, a little louder, and he waved.

"And finally," Brack said, "Dotty Drake, one of the finest magician's assistants to ever grace this theater in its heyday."

Dotty jumped to her feet. She was sitting on the aisle quite close to the stage. The crowd went wild with applause.

The three performers, all dressed in their finest show clothes, climbed the stage and joined Brack at the lectern.

"Theopolis would like us to believe that he is the greatest magician of all time," Brack said. "He'd like us to believe that he can do alone what most of us need help to do."

Theopolis backed away from the stage a little.

"This is a shame," Brack went on, "because Theopolis is a fine illusionist, and a true master of modern magic." Brack smiled and shrugged shyly. "I admit, most of his special effects go right over my old head," he added. The audience chuckled.

"But when he needed help in his schemes," Brack said, his face going serious, "he knew he'd need help from these three."

The other three performers on stage took a bow.

"Thursday here was the juggler we all saw over the pool," Brack explained. "He dressed in a robe just like Theopolis's, and the two switched places."

"It was easy in the crowd and the smoke," Charlie said, glaring at Theopolis.

"Of course," Brack went on, "Thursday wasn't actually over the pool. He was hidden away, with Madagascar and Theopolis."

Madagascar looked at his feet.

"It was Madagascar's mirrors that made Thursday appear to be levitating," Brack said. "And it was Theopolis's projector that made Thursday appear to be over the pool."

"The smoke again," Charlie said. "It was thick and white enough to act as a screen."

"And Dotty," Brack said, "the assistant, simply made sure everything went off without a hitch. She operated the smoke machine, very likely, and aimed the projector."

Dotty nodded.

When Brack's explanation was complete, the crowd cheered.

HOW THEOPOLIS'S TRICK WORKED

Projection on
smoke clouds

Mirror

Projector

Thursday
disguised
as Theopolis

"Your applause should be directed toward these four performers," Brack said. "Not me." He waved at Theopolis, calling him onstage. "It was a wonderful illusion," Brack said gently.

Theopolis slowly joined the others in the center of the stage.

"And now, our show can begin," Brack said. "I will go backstage and prepare, and these four will be . . . my opening act."

He winked at Theopolis and disappeared into the wings.

To open, Theopolis and the others performed a repeat of the trick from the party, without the pool.

No one was very impressed this time, but all of the magicians clapped hard to cheer for Mr. Thursday, Mr. Madagascar, and Dotty Drake.

By the time they were done, Brack — now fully Abracadabra — was dressed.

He stepped onto the stage. The stage lights went black, and the spotlight thumped on again and shined on the greatest **magician** in history.

Abracadabra then performed an illusion so great, so brilliant, and so completely unexplainable, that the finest minds in the world are still trying to figure out just how he did it.

Of course, Charlie knows.

ABOUT THE AUTHOR

MICHAEL DAHL grew up reading everything he could find about his hero Harry Houdini, and worked as a magician's assistant when he was a teenager. Even though he cannot disappear, he is very good at escaping things. Dahl has written the popular Library of Doom series, the Dragonblood books, and the Finnegan Zwake series. He currently lives in the Midwest in a haunted house.

ABOUT THE ILLUSTRATOR

LISA K. WEBER is an illustrator currently living in Oakland, California. She graduated from Parsons School of Design in 2000 and then began freelancing. Since then, she has completed many print, animation, and design projects, including graphic novelizations of classic literature, character and background designs for children's cartoons, and textiles for dog clothing.

DISCUSSION QUESTIONS

1. Explain Theopolis's trick. How did he do it?

2. Have you seen a magic show? Talk about some of the tricks you saw.

3. Would you want to stay at the Abracadabra Hotel? Why or why not?

WRITING PROMPTS

1. Try writing one of the chapters in this book from Brack's point of view. How does the story change? What does Brack see, hear, think, and feel?

2. Create your own magic trick. What is it? How does it work?

3. Theopolis relies on help from other magicians to do his magic trick. Write about a time you needed help from someone else to do something.

GLOSSARY

challenge (CHAL-uhnj)—to invite a person to try to do something, or to fight

concession (kuhn-SESH-uhn)—in a concession speech, someone admits that his or her opponent has won

duplicate (DOO-pluh-kate)—copy

engulfed (in-GUHLFD)—surrounded

illusion (i-LOO-zhuhn)—something that appears to exist or happen but does not

levitation (lev-i-TAY-shuhn)—the act of rising in the air and floating

monetary (MON-uh-tair-ee)—having to do with money

resident (REZ-uh-duhnt)—a person who lives in a particular place

retire (ri-TIRE)—stop working

stagehand (STAYJ-hand)—a person who works behind the scenes in a theater

THE CRAZY COMICAL SOCK

The best way to warm up an audience is to get them laughing. With this trick, the audience gets a good laugh when you find something you didn't even know was lost!

You need: Two identical socks, a piece of black cloth, a black hat, and four safety pins

PREPARATION:

1. First, pin the black cloth into the bottom of the hat to create a secret pocket as shown. Then tuck a sock into the secret pocket.

2. Next, put the other sock on your right foot. Leave your left foot bare under your shoe as shown.

PERFORMANCE:

3. Start by telling the audience that you often find the strangest things in your hat. Say, "I never know what I might get when I do this trick." Then hold the hat up to show the audience that it's empty.

4. Now wave your magic wand over the hat and say a few mysterious magic words.

5. Reach into the hat and pull out the sock. Make a funny, confused look on your face. The audience will think something went wrong.

6. While looking confused, lift your right pant leg to show the matching sock. Then quickly lift your left pant leg to show that the sock is missing. Act surprised or embarrassed — as if you made the sock appear in the hat by mistake. The audience will have a good laugh and enjoy the rest of the show!

Like this trick? Learn more in the book Amazing *Magic Tricks: Expert Level* by Norm Barnhart!
All images and text © 2009 Capstone Press. Used by permission.

CHECK IN TO THE HOCUS POCUS HOTEL

FIND MORE:
GAMES, PUZZLES, HEROES, VILLAINS, AUTHORS, ILLUSTRATORS AT...

www.capstonekids.com

Still want MORE? Find cool websites and more books like this one at www.Facthound.com. Just type in the Book ID 9781434241023 and you're ready to go!